ISBN: 978-0-692-89771-351495

Story and Script:
J.B. Butcher

Illustrations, Cover Design, Page Layout:
Zach Wideman, www.widemanillustrations.com

Written by J.B. Butcher

Illustrated by Zach Wideman

Edited by Jared Glover

A portion of the proceeds goes towards
the protection of the wild horses of North America

This book is dedicated to J. Morgan Davis. Thank you for sharing your vision about a koala bear and a wild horse that go on adventures in the OBX. I hope you enjoy!

-J.B. Butcher

Facebook: Corolla Bear

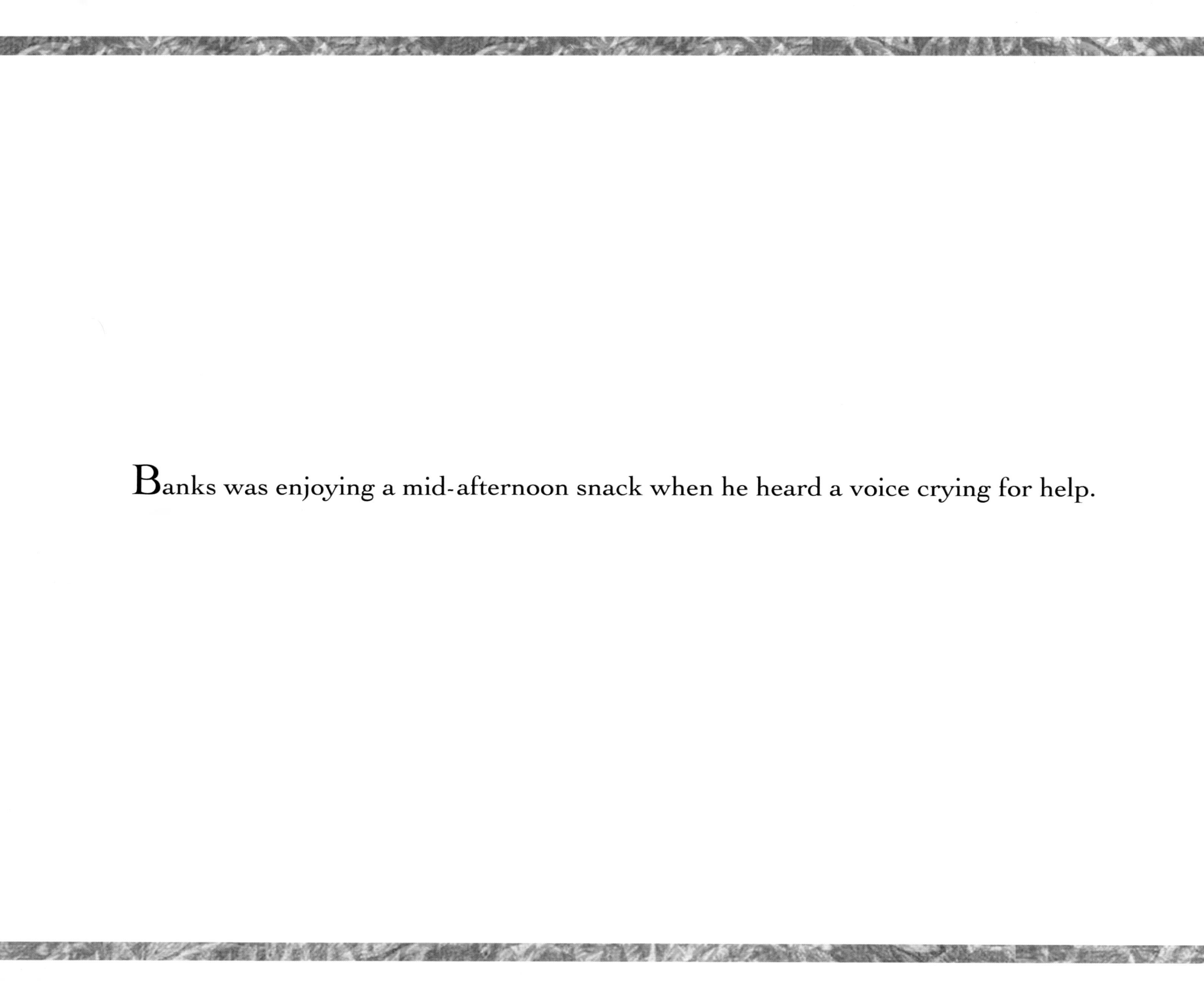

Banks was enjoying a mid-afternoon snack when he heard a voice crying for help.

Banks looked up and saw a bear stuck in a tree hanging by a parachute.
"Get me down!" cried the bear.

"How did you get stuck in a tree?" asked Banks.

"It's a long story, mate, but I'll keep it short. I'm from Australia and I decided to go on vacation because I needed a change from sitting around eating Eucalyptus leaves all day. I needed an adventure, mate, so I came to the Outer Banks of North Carolina. And for my first adventure in the OBX, I decided to go sky diving."

"Everything was fine, until a gust of wind caused me to lose control of my parachute..."

Morton

"...and I got stuck on this here tree." Banks galloped over to the tree and began shaking it, but nothing happened.

"Try unhooking yourself!" shouted Banks.
"It's too high, mate, I don't have anything to land on!"

"Land on me!"

The bear closed his eyes, unhooked himself, and fell from the tree.

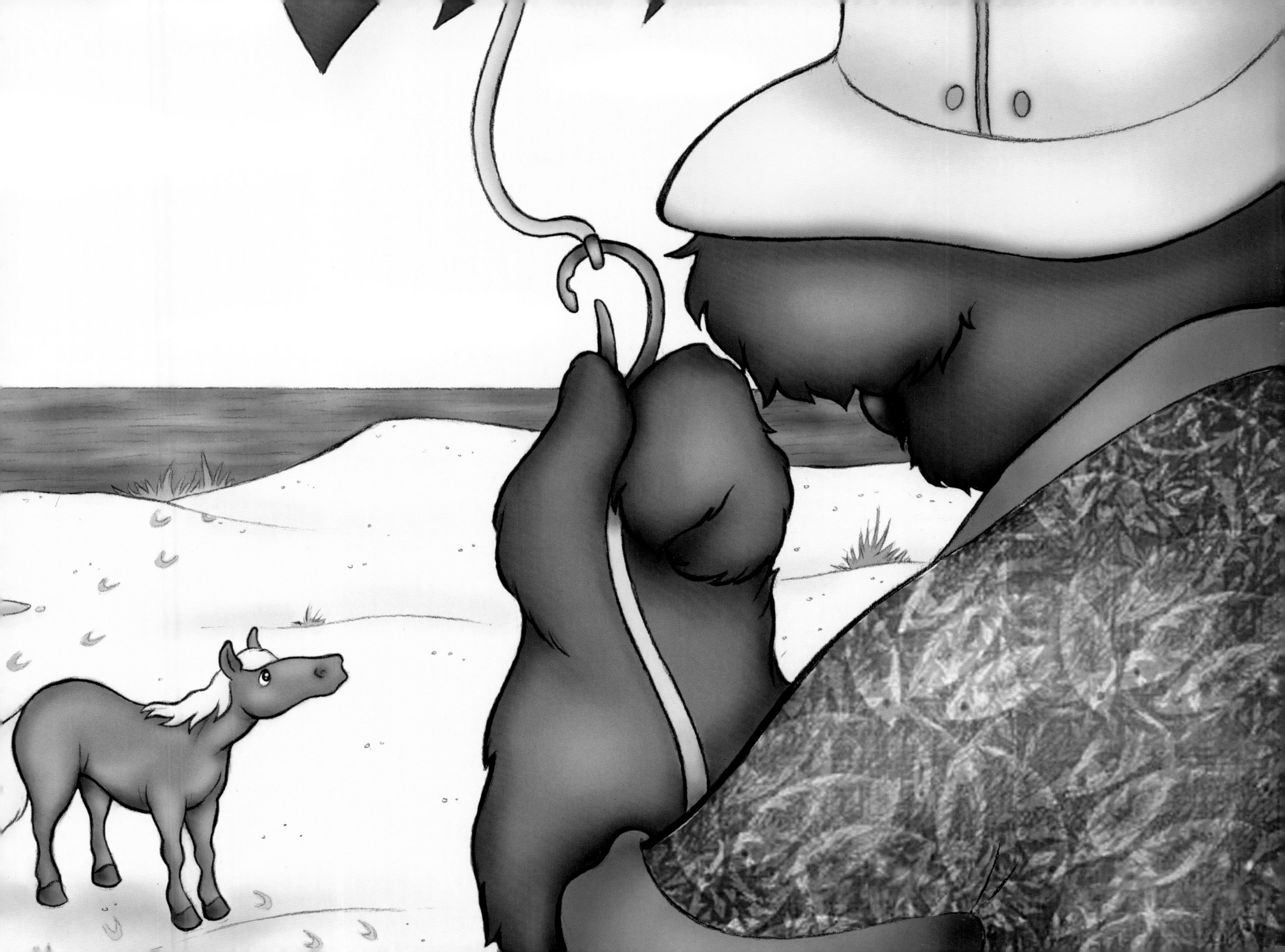

"Nice catch."

"The name's Banks, and I am the great, great, great, great, great, great, great—"

"Spit it out, mate."

"Great grandson of Estaban El Grande. What's your name?"

"Aloisha-eucalicious-straussenburg."

Banks paused for a moment. "How about we call you Corolla Bear?"

"I love it! I've always wanted a nickname."

"One day a ship set sail from Spain to visit America. The ship was packed with supplies and a group of the finest horses. One of them being Estaban El Grande."

EL MUNDO

"The journey was long and difficult for the sailors and horses.
They ran out of both food and water, and the horses were so hungry
that they began eating anything in sight. But that was just the beginning."

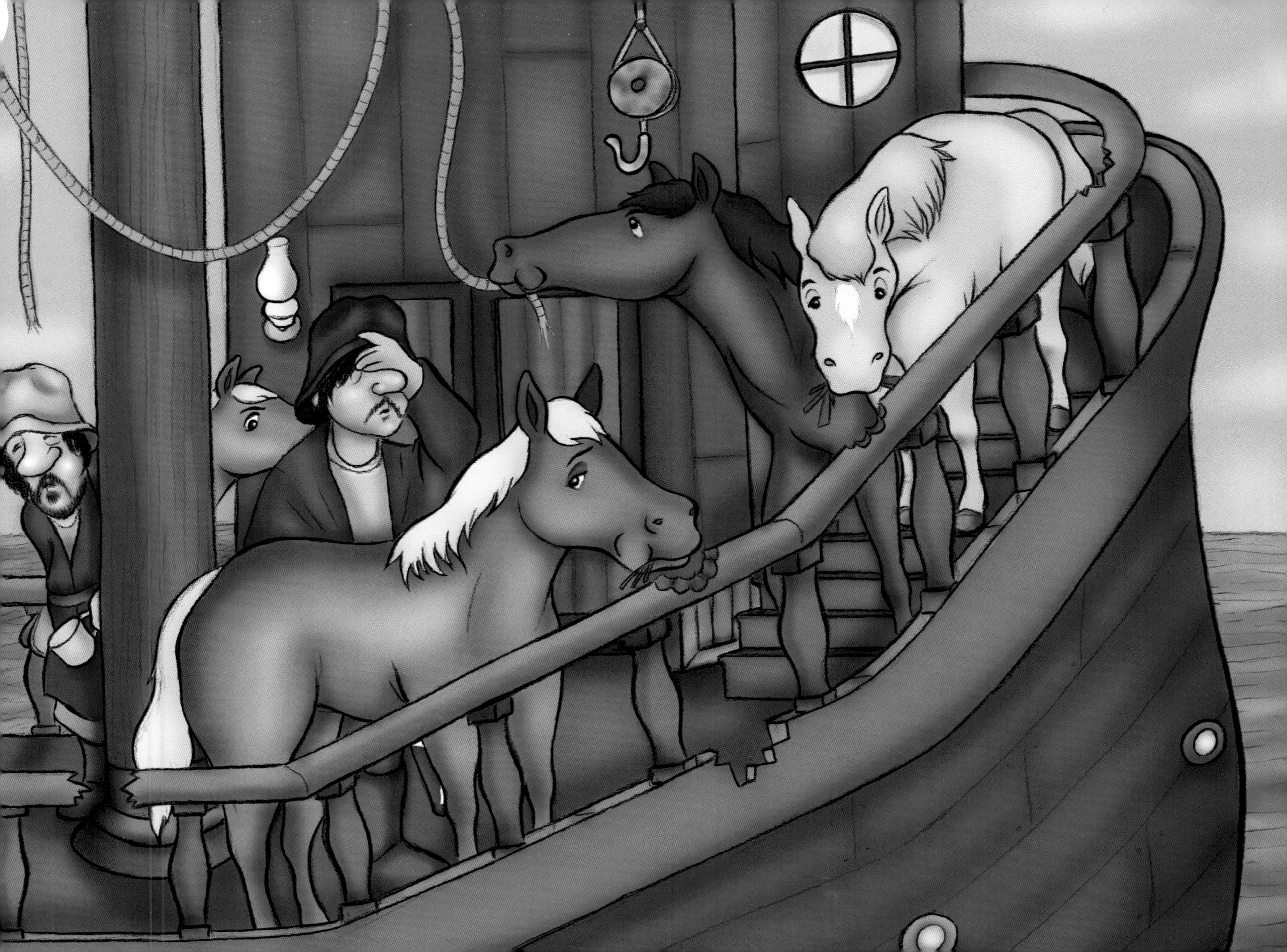

"The currents became rocky and powerful as they were getting closer to the OBX. The sailors and horses looked in the distance and saw dark clouds marching in the sky towards them."

"And as the clouds began to march overhead, lightning zipped across the sky. It was the greatest thunderstorm any one had ever seen! Waves were as high as twenty ships!"

"The thunder pounded like a massive earthquake in the sky, which shook the ship! All the horses became frightened and tried to scurry to the rear of the ship, but a single rope tied them together. And in the middle of that rope was Estaban El Grande! He planted his feet into the sopping wet wood and stared the storm in the eye!"

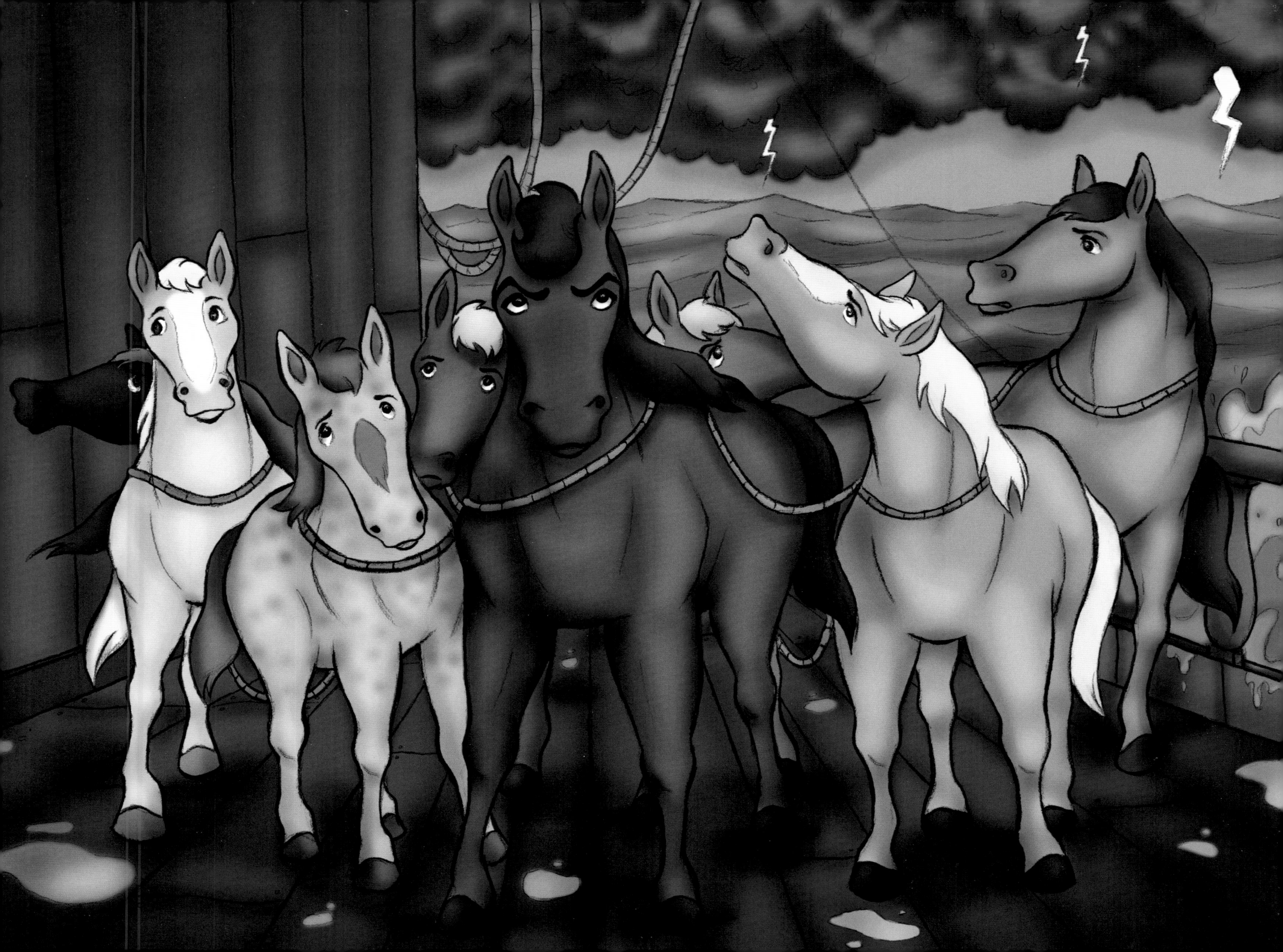

"But even the strength of Estaban's hooves were no match for this thunderstorm! Waves crashed into the ship, destroying it to pieces!"

"All was lost except for the horses, bound together by a single rope! The horses tried to swim back to the rubbage, but Estaban convinced them otherwise. 'There's no going back! The ship has sunk! Come together my friends for we can swim, not as many, but as one!' said Estaban.

"Through the mighty crashing waves and the pelting rain that stung like a wasp, Estaban and the horses swam towards OBX!"

"The horses became tired and could not swim any farther. 'It's over,"
cried one horse. 'We're doomed!' yelled another one. But Estaban
was determined to defeat this thunderstorm, for it was his greatest
battle ever! 'Forward!' yelled Estaban as he dragged the other
horses through the suction of the currents.

"The deep sound of his voice shook the tired horses and they began to once again swim with their leader. 'Shoreline ahead!' yelled Estaban."

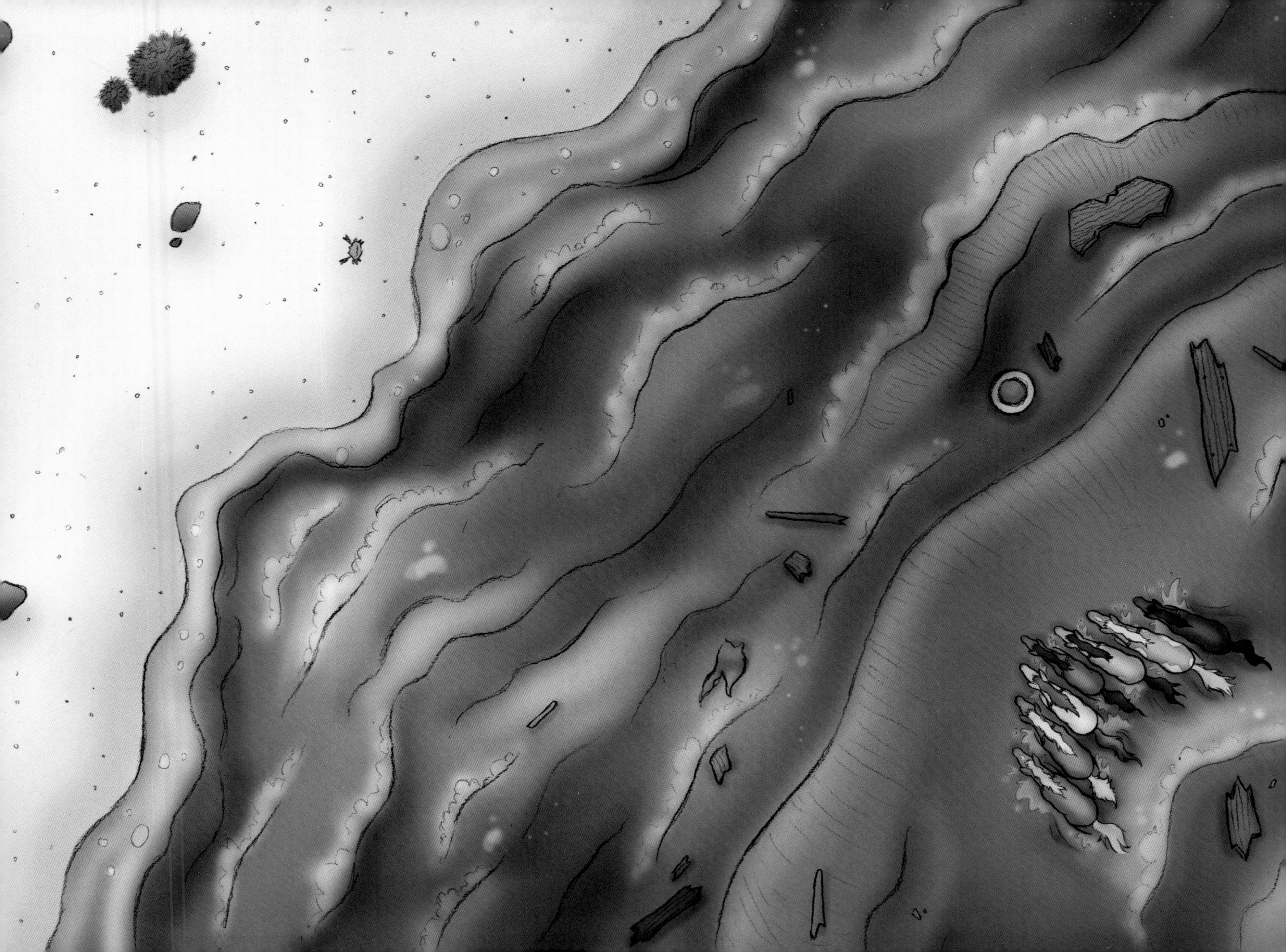

"But just as they saw the shoreline, a wave like no other began to form. Estaban sensed danger and his stomach began to curl, but he was not about to let fear get the best of him."

"The wave grew to a hundred ships high! And all Estaban
could do is look up at what might be his final battle,
while the other horses scurried away in fear."

"But Estaban, not knowing defeat, turned around and swam ...
pulling the other horses into the crashing wave!"

"The wave knocked the horses out, but fortunately for the horses, the storm was gone. The sun peaked through the clouds, peeling open Estaban's eyes. He looked around at his unconscious comrades, and knew he had to do something before they drowned."

"Tired, hungry, and thirsty, Estaban let out a loud whinny, 'Naaaaaaaaaaaay,' and began to pull the entire weight of the other horses."

"And once they got to the shoreline, Estaban untied the rope, freeing his fellow comrades."

"Then he climbed to the top of a wrecked ship and stared at his fallen comrades. So many things went through his head, but he knew he had to say something to give the other horses hope of survival on this new land."

"'Rise my brothers and sisters!' yelled Estaban. The vibration of his voice woke the other horses. And like the thunder rolling in the sky, the greatest horse ever spoke..."

'The journey to this land was difficult, but not impossible! For we overcame hunger, thirst, and a terrible thunderstorm! If we survived the journey, then surely we can survive on this land! Nothing is impossible if we stick together as one!' The horses whinnied and ever since that day we have survived on the Outer Banks."

"Wow, mate!" said Corolla Bear. "Makes me wish I could travel back in time, and meet the great Estaban El Grande."

Banks started galloping as fast as he could.

"Whoa! Where are you taking me?"

"There's an old wishing well that might be able to help."

To be continued...

Morjon

J.B. Butcher is a longtime resident of the Carolinas. He loves animals, the beach, and has a great sense of adventure. His favorite thing to do in the Outer Banks is to spend time with family and friends along with seeing the wild horses at sunrise. Currently, he writes through his company, Shoe Shine Productions.